JOHNS HOPKINS: POETRY AND FICTION
John T. Irwin, General Editor

What
the Darkness
Proposes

What
the Darkness
Proposes

Poems by
Charles Martin

The Johns Hopkins
University Press
Baltimore and London

This book has been brought to publication with the generous
assistance of the Albert Dowling Trust.

The Johns Hopkins University Press
2715 North Charles Street
Baltimore, Maryland 21218-4319
The Johns Hopkins Press Ltd., London

Library of Congress Cataloging-in-Publication Data will be found
at the end of this book.
A catalog record for this book is available from the British Library.

ISBN 0-8018-5487-3

For Leslie

The serpent that Eve once turned a flat rock to
uncover
Had only one message: Commencement means starting
over.
A second-hand shop was our first parents' endeavor.

Contents

I

II

III

I

For a Child of Seven,
Taken by the Jesuits

The little criminal is seized and shaken
Like a globe of snow; locked in a place without
Light or supper, he'd rather have been taken
By the red Indians he's read about
In Classic Comic Books; there the precocious
Seven-year-old absorbed atrocities
Of line and color scarcely less atrocious
Than the events themselves: Alice on her knees
In the glum forest, facing death or worse
From Magua, empurpled in his rage,
While those who love her ignorantly traverse
The awkward contours of a far-off page
Through thick and thin, through smudgy and grotesque:
A tightly rolled-up scroll on Father's desk.

Breaking Old Ground

What was it that roughed up and threw away
The children's toy, this plastic dinosaur
I found early this morning, where it lay
Forgotten in the muck of my backyard,
Still half-embedded in the oozy clay?
Softening winter left it stunned: it tottered
Awkwardly, until I got it to stand
On the palm and fingers of my upturned hand.

2/

Whatever took it took it by surprise,
With feline cunning or a childish shriek,
Before it could inform its painted eyes
And its impersonally molded beak
With an expression that would terrorize:
This one would not have turned the other cheek.
Yet here I found it in the slush, still grinning
At what had taken it and sent it spinning.

3/

Thinlidded eyes and sharply pointed teeth
Made a mask equal to the ironies
That oversaw the lizard's coming forth,
Its form emerging out of melting ice
After some power deep within the earth
Had fluttered those lids, tickled those ivories,
And heaved the frost that managed the displacement
Of this emissary from the basement—

4/

Or had that grin begun to find its shape
While the poor relations all were losing theirs
In transformations they could not escape?
Over the next few hundred million years
They oozed into oil, drop by viscous drop,
Until one day there suddenly appears
This obliging lump, battered but unsubdued
After one last refinement of the crude. . . .

5/

A raspberry fanfare, then, to welcome this
Adventitious charmer, well-cast spell,
This much-diminished metamorphosis
Of the great futilities that rose and fell
So many ages ago! Perhaps I'll miss
Its soiled acrylic presence (How can I tell?)
When I put it back where it was found and leave,
Ignoring the urgent tugging at my sleeve;

6/

Why should we feel obliged to, when we find
Something we haven't lost and have no need for?
Is it our desire for the ties that bind,
However loosely knotted? Or does *it* plead for
Recognition, acceptance—was it designed
To have its own designs on us? Indeed, for
It really seems to care (Though how can it say?)
Whether it's pocketed or thrown away,

7/

It really seems to want to be our friend,
Returning, is it, out of sympathy,

Or just to see how everything will end?
Waiting, in either case, for one like me
To show up some morning at the backyard fence,
A perfect stranger: who may or may not be
Impressed with what it was or where it's been,
But, taken with or by it, takes it in.

Victoria's Secret

Victorian mothers instructed their daughters, ahem,
That whenever their husbands were getting it off on them,
The only thing for it was just to lie perfectly flat
And try to imagine themselves out buying a new hat;
So, night after night, expeditions grimly set off,
Each leaving a corpse in its wake to service the toff
With the whiskers and whiskey, the lecherous ogre bent
Over her, thrashing and thrusting until he was spent
Or so we imagine, persuaded that our ancestors
Couldn't have been as brightly unbuttoned as we are,
As our descendents will shun the kinds of repression
They think we were prone to, if thinking come back into
                              fashion.
And here is *Victoria's Secret*, which fondly supposes
That the young women depicted in various poses
Of complaisant negligence somehow or other reveal
More than we see of them: we're intended to feel
That this isn't simply a matter of sheer lingerie,
But rather the baring of something long hidden away
Behind an outmoded conception of rectitude:
Liberation appears to us, not entirely nude,
In the form of a fullbreasted nymph, implausibly slim,
Airbrushed at each conjunction of torso and limb,
Who looks up from the page with large and curious eyes
That never close: and in their depths lie frozen
The wordless dreams shared by all merchandise,
Even the hats that wait in the dark to be chosen.

Tonight's Jeopardy

"This ancient author is said to have died when
an eagle dropped a tortoise on his head."

"Who was . . . John Milton?"

That question, wildly ricocheting, travels
Throughout the empyrean's upper levels
Before it knocks a tortoise off the shelf
Where it had once paused to collect itself;

It now commences free fall—has it found
The head that it will rhyme with on the ground?
Not yet, not yet: contestant number two,
A young mother of four from Kalamazoo,

Draws hope and sustenance and from thin air
A link between the tortoise and a hare
That does not hold: *"Who was . . . Aesop?" "No. . . ."*
We're left hanging for a moment or so

(Contestant number three is out to lunch
And will not try his luck or play a hunch),
While answer seeks the question still to come
And tortoise drops toward an unwitting dome

Fringed with white hair, an inexpressive mask
Weathered by questions we no longer ask,
A name our three contestants fail to guess:
"Who was the tragic poet Aeschylus?"

Souvenirs of the Late War

Now stand at ease where they (and we) once quivered
Anticipating payloads undelivered:
Erect, invisible, and still awaiting
The end of our passionate debating.

A Night at the Opera

Flamboyant at the end,
She has her sister send
For Aeneas once more—
One last time, before
She turns from the wall
To give the death scene all
She has, her sullen passion
Become a sharp weapon.
Spare, merciless and quick,
That self-hating rhetoric
Lifts the flesh from her bones
And partially atones
For some of her past folly.
—That Queen, that poor duped dolly,
Stripped now of all but her
Speech, rises to the pure
Outrage of poetry,
Triumphant, even as he
Flees—who will never return,
Whom she cannot hope to burn
In the fiery crucible
Of her chastened will.
And having had her say,
She torches her life away:
Flames quiver at her lips.

On one of the adamant ships
Already lost to sight,
He thinks ahead: tonight
He will not have a woman.

Already a good Roman,
Thoroughly sick of the sea,
He thinks of how easily
The strongest walls are shaken,
How cities may be taken
By cleverness, by force—
Recalling the wooden horse
And the breech made in the wall,
He says, to no one at all,
"No fundament of stone
Is safe to build upon;
My city will be made
Of Law; my laws obeyed;
In my earth-wracking city
Will be no room for pity
Or weakness of any kind;
Strict Justice, who is blind,
And angry Mars will keep
My city when I rule,
And after, when I sleep—
A thousand years or more,
Two thousand years before . . ."

Those ardent embers cool.

Getting the Miracle Wrong

The stale, essential snowflake which was said
To be Christ's body, our Wonder Bread,
Stuck and then melted on my outthrust tongue—
That seemed a miracle. When I was young,
It happened every time I went to Mass.
But as the priest explained it to our class,
Displaying an unconsecrated crumb
Between his right-hand forefinger and thumb,
"The miracle's that *this* becomes Our Savior—"

Not that the bread was wholly without flavor.

Flying Heads

Lopped off, they jetted wings at shoulder level
A moment after their brief lives were ended;
Skittering from the clutches of the Devil,
The little ones ascended

In formation to surround Our Savior
And fan the victors of the Church Triumphant.
Cited on the field for good behavior,
Each newly halo'd infant

Fusses and fidgets, waiting for the Day
Of Judgement, when the dead will all be sifted,
And those who've been naughty will be led away
While the righteous are uplifted . . .

Artists would afterwards enjoy devising
Improvements on that model—if a second
Pair of wings would aid in stabilizing
Erratic flybabies, they reckoned

That a third pair would be even better:
Two wings prone, two supine, two akimbo,
According to the spirit or the letter
Of the law in Limbo,

Where some had been consigned by their Creator.
In Limbo is Latin, meaning *on the border:*
There, tiny passengers whose elevator
Has gone out of order

Wait between floors now on their way to heaven:
Some pressing noses against the emergency button,
Some hanging upside down like bats in a cavern—
Not remembered, not forgotten.

Beauty

(G. G. Belli, "La Bbellezza")

Beauty is God's most perfect gift, a present
Better than money, as reflection teaches,
For money can't make beautiful what isn't,
While those with beauty will acquire riches.

A church, a cow, a girl—it's true, my friend,
The ugly ones don't get a second look;
And God himself, of Wisdom without end,
Sought beauty in the mother that he took.

No door is ever locked that beauty sees,
And everyone makes eyes at it, although
Its faults are noted—with apologies.

Your cat had kittens, friend? Those with the cutes
Are those that get kept: ugly kittens go
Off to the dump, unlucky little brutes.

Death with a Coda

(G. G. Belli, "La Morte Co La Coda")

You're either a Christian or a Liberal,
Those are the choices: there aren't any more;
If Christian, whether you're a slob or swell,
Death is a step that chills you to the core.

Run off to a party or the latest show,
Hang out in taverns, give the girls a poke,
Go into business—make yourself some dough;
Then, when you've got your little bundle . . . croak.

Next comes the afterlife, which you attend
Like school without vacation—what a curse!
It lasts for always and will never end.

What drives me crazy is the thought of *never!*
Afloat or at bottom, for better or for worse,
That bitch eternity goes on forever!

The Two of Them

But no, it isn't over for them yet:
They sit off by themselves, watching the sun set
   Behind the hills striated now with fog.
Two coffees, one forbidden cigarette:

They pass at intervals its glowing coal
From each to other. Pressed sheets of fog roll
   Into the valley right before a range
Of hills like mountains in a Chinese scroll,

Where fog is something dreamt of by the ocean
Beyond, a post-impressionist's impression
   Of large and little waves all pressing shoreward,
And quietly dispersing in slow motion

A few last smudgy bits of broken light:
The distant range had kept this out of sight.
   Seeing beyond it was beyond them both,
Who saw no further than the coming night,

The room that would be there as certainly
As was the ocean which they could not see;
   And in that room, all they would first remember
And afterwards imagine, when memory

Would no more lift a fingertip to trace
Out of the darkness, contours of a face
   Or gestures that imperceptibly once led
Into the fierce constrictions of embrace:

Persistence of the gestures that renew
Desire is the legend woven through
    Those days and nights, now to be read only
Here in what I have written of these two,

Who sit where I have put them and think about
The way it goes from certainty to doubt
    And back again until the coffee's cold
And the glowing coal is carefully stubbed out.

They leave tomorrow, taking what is theirs.
A sky magnificently shot with stars
    Has been arranged tonight to bring them in
As the last slip of sunlight disappears

Beyond the hills; and while coyotes howl
Their heartsick threnodies, a Great Horned Owl
    Gives answers to the questions that she poses
And then soars into darkness on the prowl.

The Philosopher's Balloon

Whether the Laws that govern us were fashioned
For our benefit (who otherwise
Might find ourselves in the breathless stratosphere)
Or were meant to keep us from our rightful station
Remains unsettled, open to surmise—
But that there *are* Laws is absolutely clear.
We derive the existence of these Laws
Not from the necessity of a First Cause,
Some creator inflating us until we squeal,
But from the strings to which we are attached,
Which represent the Laws and those who make them;
That the strings attached to us are really real,
And not, as some say, just a figure of speech,
Becomes apparent only when we break them.

II

A Walk in the Hills
above the Artists' House

I   Neither Here nor There

1/

Late afternoon: in studios
Where work is done or unbegun,
Disoriented poets close
The books on rough draft or revision;
Outside, as a declining sun
Takes aim at the Pacific Ocean,
A little clearing slowly fills
With those who'd like to walk the hills

2/

Above the temporary quarters
(Emptying out now for the hike)
Where composers, artists, writers
Have settled in to make their mark,
Each different but all alike
In having gotten time to work
As much or little as we please,
And walk sometime among the trees

3/

Perhaps the same trees I flew over
After I managed to exchange
My sweaty feedbag for the clover
Of a few weeks' idleness;
Significant others find it strange,
But work that any artist does

23

Paradoxically depends
On leisure to achieve its ends.

4/

So here I am in my new cell,
Which might belong to anyone;
There's little that it has to tell
About the others who've passed through:
Wisps of patchouli linger on,
But no more urgent residue
Of effort, concentration, doubt—
No marks gouged in, no butts ground out,

5/

No sign of work brought to conclusion
By any former resident
Or left to trail off in confusion. . . .
A womb in which *I* may conceive,
Supportive yet indifferent,
It will recover when I leave,
And someone else, when I'm *not* here—
But wait a moment! I just got here:

6/

A week ago, in some suspense,
I'd driven up a golden coast
Past signs that threatened ARMED RESPONSE,
Straining my rent-a-wreck until—
Have I gone past it? Am I lost?
—A grand museum on a hill
Presented itself: with the view
I caught a glimpse of *deja vu:*

7/

My eyes if not my legs had been
(How did I know it?) Here before:
A gate, a guard who let me in
To find the underground garage:
An elevator rose one floor
And opened up on a mirage;
I knew the place—and stood amazed
At the great villa Piso raised!

8/

Piso, the Getty of his time
(Both men had made it big in oil),
Who built at Herculaneum
A summer refuge from the dreary
Round of urban stress and toil,
His *Villa dei—Che? Papiri!*
The name applied to it much later
By an Italian excavator,

9/

Who found the room where Philodemus,
Philosopher in minor key,
Elaborated his great theme
In essay and in epigram;
Praised the mysterious faculty
For which he had no proper name:
Imagination, understood
As any art's supremest good.

10/

Vesuvius cried, "Hold that thought!"
And all his wit and eloquence,
Unread, unheard of, lay unsought;

Oblivion's new underground
Poet and scholar in residence
(Alas!) was nowhere to be found,
Until a pickaxe let in light
On notions long kept out of sight:

11/

Leaves of his Book, reduced to ash
And shoveled from a cluttered shelf,
Were almost thrown out with the trash:
"Oh—were those *scrolls?*" Now blackened lace.
At first uncertain of itself,
Each inkstained fragment finds a place;
There are few guides for the perplexed
When charred briquets become a text,

12/

And text becomes a voice that lifts
Off from its backing to present
Us with long-unaccustomed gifts;
Here Philodemus criticizes
Artists who merely represent,
Then asks a question that surprises:
"Why can't a painter paint instead
A man with, say, a horse's head?

13/

"Why can't he show us, if he wishes,
A human face upon a creature
With a tail just like a fish's?
Why must an artist be confined
To drawing images from nature,
Ignoring those that spring from mind?"

So, in a cell provided him
By Piso's will or Piso's whim,

14/

The poet artfully composed
In well-funded isolation;
Who did not own himself, proposed
The right of artists to create,
Each from his own imagination,
Rather than merely imitate;
"For, as we grasp in our dreams,
The world is hardly what it seems.

15/

"As our poets all inform us,
In poetry false may be true,
Great may be small, and small, enormous;
The fabulous is natural:
Cyclops complaining of the view
And Venus on her scallop shell
May have originated in a
Cheese that Piso served at dinner. "

16/

Poets had little, Piso, plenty;
He loved the prestige that accrued
To him among the cognoscenti
Who fattened on his patronage;
How could his mansion *not* include
A room for his residing sage?
As well as one for pinky rings
And for the girlfriends' slinky things.

The villa Piso built was soon
Unfit for *any* occupant;
It disappeared one afternoon
Under a flow of laval silt
That hardened into adamant.
I walked through one that had been built
In imitation of its plan
By a wealthy Californian,

Then drove to the artists' colony
Much farther north—the inspiration
Of a modern mage whose alchemy
Resulted in *la pilule d'or,*
Which helped free sex from generation,
And made a large non-profit for
The foundation on whose real estate
I am ensconced now to create.

And where, last night, we met our host,
Who did his best to break the ice
Between the salad and the roast:
"It seems to me the life you chose
Is a continual sacrifice
That you've accepted; yet, suppose
The work you did could find no venue—
Would you be willing to continue

"If you could have no hope of any
Response from anyone at all,
Have neither fame nor love nor money,

Nor yet the thumbscrew nor the rack,
And—this, I think, would most appall
Even indifference held back;
Given a worst-case scenario
Out of Beckett, Kafka, Poe—

21/

"Immured in some grim *oubliette*
Whence word of you would never issue,
And none there were who would regret
Your absence from the banquet table,
Or call you up to say, 'We miss you!'
Is it—I mean—would you be able,
Could you create, without the sense
Your work had use or consequence?"

22/

Good question. Once a poet-friend
Told me that if he ever heard
The world was coming to an end—
The missile launched with his name on it—
He'd try to put in a last word
Or two on an unfinished sonnet.
Although I think that I would try to
Find someone to say good-bye to,

23/

It is a personal decision
As to whether, at closing time,
The life or work most wants revision—
I can't do other than admire
His quest for one last, perfect rhyme,
Such a fierce refining fire—

I guess I ought to make it clear
I mean the poet's fire, here—

24/

But if our writing matters, what
Makes it matter matters more
Than *it* does—what goes on without,
In inexpressively tremendous
Regions of after and before
And happening right now, beyond us—
All that we simply do not get.
It promises us nothing, yet

25/

My poet-friend would have in mind
A saving grace to end up with,
As I would too—I'd hope to find
An image suitably oblique:
The unilluminated moth
That fluttered from an opened book
And struggles to ascend on air
Will soon be neither here nor there.

II   Letter from Here for Now

1/

You ask me to describe the way
I live out here—is there a routine
That I've established for my stay,
And do I have a cell or suite,
Who are the others on the scene,
And the cooking—is it fit to eat?
Important questions, which one guest will
Try to answer in this epistle.

30

2/

I'll start at the alarming break
Of day, when I am least productive:
Some of us slowly come awake,
While others leap and prance like goats;
The difference can be instructive
If you're alert and taking notes,
Which I am usually not.
I take a shower (very hot),

3/

Then amble to the kitchen, where
A neighbor infinitely kind
Is just beginning to prepare
A breakfast for however many
Rise to its bait. "Charles, look behind
Those cans and see if we've got any
More Bisquick left."
               The mix is found,
And obdurate dark beans are ground

4/

Into a silt that, drop by drop,
First holds its liquor, then releases
A brew that makes the spoon stand up;
And, as my neighbor briskly stirs
Three kinds of freshly grated cheeses
With *funghi,* peahen eggs, and herbs
Snipped from a teeming window box,
I slice bagels and shave the lox

5/

Into such sheer transparencies
As an optician might well use

For rosy-colored eyeglass lenses:
A salt-and-salmon-flavored tint.
Some minor touches and we're through;
Sliced oranges are dressed with mint,
The table with a fresh bouquet
Of wildflowers. . . .

                    What's that you say?

6/

"This man is mad, or else a liar!"
Well, my description represents
The breakfast to which I aspire,
Our dailiness idealized—
As anyone with any sense
Would long ago have realized.
Some days *are* special—but on most
Others it's cereal or toast,

7/

A cup of coffee, then a second
Which I take back into my study.
By now I've pretty much awakened,
I'm sitting at my writing table
With pencils sharpened, notebook ready:
"Baker, Baker, this is Able. . . . "
Then words come tumbling in a flood
Or one by one like drops of blood,

8/

Or sometimes none at all, depending.
In finding what there is to say,
In sitting, quietly attending,
Until *they're* there, between blue lines:
Then letting them go on their way

Or fitting them to my designs
In the sweet exercise of will,
Unbroken hours pass, until

9/

Through thin walls I hear my neighbors
On either side decide, "We're done!"
And me? I've little for my labors.
Four lines that seem less than terrific:
"Outside as a declining sun
Takes aim at [*aims at?*] the Pacific,
A posted notice quickly fills
With names of those who'll walk the hills. . . . "

10/

And as I join those who assemble
In the clearing, blue jays chide
The visitors that gawk and shamble,
Unlike the Californians, who
Take walks like this one in their stride
And are, by now, accustomed to
Nasturtium leaves like manhole covers
And mates who *like* their spouses' lovers;

11/

Those of us here for the first time
Find it all marvelously strange
And overdose on the sublime,
As even now my mind's eye traces
A sinuously curving range
Covered with dun-colored grasses
Below an ocean glimpsed in slivers,
Whose first appearance gave me shivers.

12/

And then got me to worrying
That all such marvels have their price:
Would work lose out to sightseeing
And vinous, late-night conversations
In this terrestrial paradise,
This ranch that raises expectations,
And where the only thing amiss
Is my concern that nothing is?

13/

Am I engaging in this blather
Merely to hide my awkwardness
As unfamiliar spirits gather?
Sojourners in-and-out-of state
Know that a question will suffice
To prompt the inarticulate,
And strangers to each others' aims
Find common ground in dropping names:

14/

No one at first knows anyone,
But this one *once* knew that one's *ex,* and
A moment later we've begun
The questioning that soon reveals
Ramifications which extend
Beyond the moment and much else,
To distant galaxies which glow
With reruns of *The Lucy Show.* . . .

15/

I'll get to know some neighbors better,
And after going on my way
I'll keep in touch by phone or letter

With first a few, then two, then one,
Until a letter sent one day
Returns to me, *address unknown.*
Or was it not sent anyhow?
But that's enough of them for now:

16/

As we set out on our walk,
I fumble the new terms, intent
On unfamiliar leaf and stalk
Expressed in Latin or in Greek
Words lifted out of what they meant
To join the English we now speak;
Fresh labels lovingly applied
By Herb, our knowledgable guide

17/

To unfamiliar plants and trees:
Here's *Artemisia,* there's *French Broom,*
That's Hemlock, sipped by Socrates;
And this bright orange-petaled mound
Is Monkeyweed, in frantic bloom;
And on the hillsides that surround,
There's growth too tall for underbrush:
Baccharis, called Coyotebush.

18/

I quickly scribble down the names
And usually a remark
Disposing of disputed claims,
As one by one, Herb settles each
Aboard the taxonomic ark
And tucks it in—then tells us which

Of them prefer to creep and crawl,
Which imitate suburban sprawl;

19/

Which cling to roadsides, which invade
The meadows and choke out old growth;
Which do best in partial shade
And which are partial to the sun,
And which impartially like both;
And in his meditation on
The brief lives of the flowers
He finds a paradigm for ours,

20/

A world like our own, comprised
Of angrily competing nations,
Of colonists and colonized.
Through vegetable eons of
Warfare, conquests, exterminations,
Too green to cry, *We've had enough*
Of all this mindless grief!
Now wait:
It's easy to exaggerate

21/

But *what* is this ungainly thing
Ahead of us? Thick limbs arrayed
In rags of bark inspiring
Legends deep-rooted in despair,
Stories of some great loser, flayed
Beyond redemption or repair,
Some Marsyas, securely bound
In great lianas: run to ground

36

22/

He found himself (so many do)
Settling down into a place
He'd only thought of passing through:
A pulse of air stirred hollow bone,
And he by metamorphosis
Became this tree, called a *Madrone*;
The name, as usual, supplied
Us in passing by our guide.

23/

What made me think of Marsyas,
Whose nerves a jealous god stripped bare?
Perhaps the heat that vaporizes
Oils of laurel, sage, and dill
And leaves them hanging in the air,
Their tangled scents a clue, until,
Though it's somewhere I've never been,
I feel I'm back in Greece again.

24/

But would Greek poets in a chorus
Transported here cry, "Hold the flutes—
Eureka, fellows—that's *Baccharis*!"
Would Aristotle find the same
Essences and attributes
Present under either name?
Would hemlock growing in these hills
Have given Socrates the chills?

25/

Is it appropriate to call
By foreign names the native rose?
And if we must give names at all,

Should haughty Dame Nomenclature
Eurocentrically impose
On the New World's unspoiled nature?
No: let our names all plainly come
From the American idiom,

26/

Speech unhoused and unhousebroken,
Speech unadorned by ornament
And understood (if not yet spoken)
By cats and dogs—even by
Poets of xenophobic bent
Who'd cast a grim, suspecting eye
On anyone who would embarrass
A native with the name *Baccharis.*

27/

Coyotebush sounds more demotic,
Though the first part is Nahuatl,
Which (to my ear) is as exotic
As is *Baccharis*—a metaphor
Not just unknown to Aristotle
But unconceived of heretofore,
Unless in the un-Aristote-
lian vision of Coyote,

28/

A trickster who has many names,
And lends *his* to anonymous
Coyotes at coyote games;
No more than two of them could fit
Underneath each eponymous
Shrub to hide from one who's "it,"

38

Huddled together jowl by cheek
In feral bouts of hide-and-seek. . . .

29/

But I—or rather, *this*—digresses,
This poem, is it, in a style
That like a summer's breeze caresses,
Touches upon, the group that passes
Over a ridge in single file,
Parting a waist-high sea of grasses
Before the sun, declining west,
And shadows, lengthening, suggest

30/

Another theme, so often used
That I was anxious to avoid it,
Afraid that I would be accused
Of terminal belatedness;
Ecclesiastes once employed it,
Borrowed, no doubt, from *Gilgamesh*:
Nothing is new under the sun,
And all is vanity we've done.

31/

Thoughts such as these often occur
As shadows pull us to the brink
Of night, and vision starts to blur;
What's left for anyone to do,
And can I freshen up that drink?
Of course you can, I wish I knew—
But is it possible that we,
Who think ourselves *le dernier cri,*

32/

And who collectively inherit
The forms all former ages shaped,
Can do no better than to parrot—
Or, as we say, "appropriate"—
Grand themes in styles once apt, now aped,
Once suitable, now second-rate?
And, as I asked before, must we
Who think ourselves *le dernier cri,*

33/

As we might say, "the latest thing"
Inhabit a formal emptiness,
Grimly diminuendo-ing
Until the end, boys—or should we
Rent us a hall and self-express,
No matter how insensibly;
"Choose now, there are no other choices,"
(This from a press of urgent voices.)

34/

Isn't it possible to choose
Neither of those? Can't we restore
The Age of Innocence? Refuse
To abide by the archaic ban
Instituted long before
The Age of Irony began?
In short, return to that forbidden
Day-Care Center known as Eden,

35/

Where our first parents make their way
On paths that wind through cunning mazes
In which their clueless footsteps stray;

Now pausing to consult the *Guide
To Hosannas, Hymns, and Praises*
(A book the Gideons provide);
Or wondering, beneath a tree,
What to put on for company.

36/

But they're so easily delighted,
Who have no prospects that displease—
Imagine them at some unsighted
Locus classicus of love,
A mossy bank, a screen of trees
Resembling this alder grove
Where two unmet before will meet
While seeking refuge from the heat.

37/

Imagine their new satisfaction!
Transparent, with no character
To propel them into action,
Uncompromised by pre-worn diction,
They simply *can't be insincere*:
Lacking most elements of fiction,
They fall back naturally on setting
As they get on with the begetting.

38/

Such getting on begets the myth
Of prelapsarian innocence
We're all of us familiar with,
And, when we fall in love, believe:
That two may put of all pretense
And every purpose to deceive,

And find, when having come together,
Themselves possessed in one another.

39/

Yet even here in paradise
Are intimations of times past,
Which our timeless myth denies:
Averted glances, words unspoken
Suggest that concord will not last,
The knot of tangled limbs be broken,
And new delight turn to dismay
With one another: while this may

40/

Be paradise, it isn't Eden.
Or is it just that they're too late?
Whether upstanding or downtrodden,
Even the grass has a history
Whose character determines fate,
Which it must bow to, as must we.
But what of [insert name here]? You,
The fiction this is written to—

41/

To whose low tastes I've often pandered,
Made insecure by your impatience—
By now, I'm sure of it, you've wandered
Off to find greater thrills and spills
Than these abstruse ruminations,
These sugar-coated quinine pills
Of mine are able to provide—
Ah, but you're here still at my side!

42/

You haven't gone at all—and even
If you *had* left me for a moment,
That's easily and soon forgiven.
But joy in your return is blended
With the renewal of this torment,
For without you I might have ended
This poem here and now, set free
From my incessant anxiety:

43/

Ambivalent are our dealings:
I summon up and soon discard
Resentment, gratitude, hurt feelings.
Nevertheless, without you, I
Might wind up in the *avante garde,*
Generic Reader   which is why
The chief complaint I have of you
Is that so far you're far too few.

44/

But now we should be going in:
While we've enjoyed our stop-time solo,
Others, invisible, have been
At work: I hear a swelling chorus
In the ranch house kitchen far below;
Dinner will be waiting for us,
But if we hurry down, I think
There may be time to have a drink,

45/

Before we gather all around
The table, headed up by Beryl,
Our English cook, who's very fond

Of serving us exotic roasts
Of flesh predominantly feral,
From local game farms or (she boasts)
The road itself: a joke, we say,
But look for skid marks anyway.

46/

And finding none, blunt hunger's edge
On what the kitchen has provided
(Possum in plum sauce with 3 veg);
Now conversations may resume,
New intimacies are confided
And circulate around the room,
Until the vocal current weakens,
And slumber, or some number, beckons.

47/

Soon those who've paired off disappear:
Where do they go? They go to town,
While the unpartnered linger here.
There comes a moment when, returning
To my own room, I lay me down
With the few lines I wrote this morning,
Racked by bouts of indecision
And second thoughts about revision,

48/

And most of all—the hour's late—
How will I bring *this* to an end?
It threatens not to terminate,
Although its day is all but over:
We've seen the sun's flat disc descend
Beyond the hills, go undercover

Preparing for its next assignment.
And so, if my announced design meant

49/

Anything, it should have meant
Closure, conclusion, *Buona sera!*
Perhaps it has its own intent,
This poem does, and now rehearses
Developments I'm unaware of,
For parthenogenetic verses
To strut to, uninhibited,
While I lie sleeping in my bed,

50/

And the few problems that still linger
(Such as the one of finding closure)
Are solved (though I don't lift a finger),
As walls and ceiling liquify
(A *stanza* slipping out of measure?)
To show the stars against the sky
Indifferent to limb and breath
As to the nothing underneath

51/

The nothingness that seems to be
An endless, unmodulated roar
Our voices must accompany—
But this is getting serious!
Doctor, I've had this dream before:
Moonlight, winter, a delirious
Traveler teetering on the edge
Of a crumbling sandstone ledge

52/

Dreams, it may be, of a way back
And goes back that way in his dream
Until he dreams himself awake
Among appearances deceiving:
Two of him there, as it would seem,
And then one evanesces, leaving
The other with—with what profound
Wisdom drawn up from underground?

53/

What is he struggling to say?
Awake, I've lost it, but I'll find
My poem on a silver tray
Beside the bed: the ink still wet,
The paper warm, the work unsigned;
Before I put my name to it,
Let me compose, in other words,
The residence that it affords:

54/

Four walls, a ceiling and a floor,
A desk, a bed, a chair or two;
One wall of glass, a sliding door
That leads onto a balcony
From which I have a lightening view
Of the low hills in front of me,
And now an ending as the sun
Rising shows a new day begun.

III *Then as it Happened*

1/

We say time passes, but we pass
And time remains. We are the motion
Of wind through levelheaded grass,
Fire that quickens the slow hill,
A cloud's shadow on the ocean;
Always we are what is unstill:
For all the length of our days
We are what passes, not what stays.

2/

Then as it happened, I flew back
Into my interrupted life,
With Beryl's box lunch in my pack:
Half of a nicely roasted hare
(Still warm when lifted off the drive)
Ripe olives, riper cheese, a pear;
A pleasing bottle of *Merlot,*
And planks of fragrant sourdough.

3/

Now I'm the envy of my flightmates,
Who stare, disconsolate, or prod
The mess of nutrients and nitrates
There on the tray before them, slowly
Congealing in a plastic pod
That swarms with virulent *E. coli.* . . .
On either side, I realize,
A traveler with hungry eyes

4/

Compels me to consume in stealth
Beryl's impressive provender,
Or open up and share the wealth:
I'm seldom one to split a hare,
And it's not easy to surrender
The last fruits of my being-there,
But how can I not? Three of us dine
Sumptuously and then recline,

5/

Before we presently withdraw
From company: *Aisle* finds his place in
Grisham's new proof of Gresham's Law,
While an expanded *Window Seat*
Dozing, mumbles, "Fortnum . . . Mason. . . . "
Alone at thirty thousand feet,
A conscious dust mote in the hand
Of powers I cannot command,

6/

I find myself revisiting
Conversations long since ended,
Revising them and editing
The balls I'd fumbled on occasion
Out of the sound-mix I'd intended;
Each irrefutable new version,
Severed from its ahem, ahems,
Glitters with aphoristic gems.

7/

Such harmless fixes and inventions
Are how we turn the tables on
Life that nixes our intentions;

The arguments we've deconstrued
When all at last is said and done,
Spring up again, revived, renewed
In thrust and parry and riposte—
Now interrupted by our host:

8/

"The moth that figures in your myth
About the end?" (Referring to
The moth I ended Part I with)
"It's altogether clear that this
Moth represents the poet, who
Is changed, just like a chrysalis—
The open book he rises from
Must mean our moth is a bookworm—

9/

"Or else the book is his cocoon—
That reading suits the image better,
For in my view, the poet's one
Who brings order to the world's waste
Bit by bit, letter by letter,
And each laboriously traced
On his own flesh, until he's dressed in
An artful weave of self-expression.

10/

"One final transformation must
See him released forevermore
From the last trace of mortal dust:
The ties that bind him to his text
Must be completely slipped, before—"
(Rilke will be decanted next,

I hear it coming) "—he roams free
In realms of pure transcendency. . . . "

11/

Interpretation is an act
Of generosity, and I
Can hardly but be grateful. Tact
And gratitude at once combine
In what I hope will satisfy:
"That figure now is yours, not mine."
A wiggle gets me off the hook.
Another reading sees the book

12/

As one that poets often get
Thrown at them by critics who
Rise up, determined not to let
Our follies unreproven go:
"Do just as *Theory* tells you to,
Obey when *History* says *no*—
And since *we're* all that matters, why
Must you keep writing poetry?

13/

"Why don't you give up? Go away!
You aren't needed anymore:
The artist is a stowaway,
Feeding upon the silken cloth
And arcane notions we import,
A houligan, a parasite—a moth!
When we eliminate this pest,
Our Emperor will be well-dressed. . . . "

14/

You're raising *that* again, I see:
Is it unfair of me to note
A certain, well, transparency
In your designs? Yet no one tries
Harder than I do: I blink and squint,
At times I've even closed both eyes—
In short, I do my level best
To see the Emperor as dressed.

15/

But something in me keeps me from
The thought that seeing is obeying.
It may be that I'm just too dumb.
It may be nothing other than
That I am most myself when playing
The obdurate contrarian
Who *will* say no, whose days are spent
Refusing to give blind assent.

16/

Not one among us without doubt
Would be at all inclined to choose
A gift one would do well without,
—Unless one *wanted* to be labeled
Obscure, archaic, and obtuse
By the much-differently-abled;
And yet this disability
Of saying what one cannot see

17/

Might have a useful application
Elsewhere, in another setting:
A space arises from negation

(A cell? A suite? Descriptions vary:
"That fireplace!" "The central heating!"
"Exotic!" "Rather ordinary . . . ")
Resistant shape, wherein one may
Imagine what one has to say,

18/

And though the many will ignore it,
As by appointment or by chance
Someone will appear before it
(For someone always has, so far)
Who'll find this measured utterance
Appealing, and (the door ajar)
Will wander in, alone, unheeding,
As to—oh, a poetry reading,

19/

Whose audience consists of . . . you.
There's only one of you, I see.
One would have hoped there might be two.
One ought to be outnumbered by
One's audience, don't you agree?
The two of us, then? You and I?
Will no one else be dropping in?
I thought as much. Then let's begin. . . .

20/

While one by one my readers find
A room to stay in for a while,
A place within the work of mind,
I dream about a group that passes
Over a ridge in single file
Parting a waist-high sea of grasses

Until our steward comes demanding
That I prepare for our landing;

21/

And in the moments that remain
Of this transcontinental flight,
I bless the powers that sustain
Us as our fragile ark descends
Toward lives we will resume tonight,
And bless the darkness that extends
Beyond us and proposes what
We will all come to, no doubt but.

III

Reflections after a Dry Spell
For Howard Nemerov

A good poet is someone who manages,
in a lifetime of standing out in thunderstorms,
to be struck by lightning five or six times.
—Randall Jarrell

And the one who took this literally
Is the one that you still sometimes see
In the park, running from tree to tree

On likely days, out to stand under
The right one *this* time—until the thunder
Rebukes him for yet another blunder. . . .

But the one who knew it was nothing more
(That flash of lightning) than a metaphor,
And said as much, as he went out the door—

Of that one, if you're lucky, you just may find
The unzapped verse or two he left behind
On the confusion between World and Mind.

Modernism: The Short Course

1/

In the beginning, it was a thin wedge that divided
  Us all along the fault line of approval,
So that we either gave our assent and applauded,
  Or else wrote letters demanding its removal.

2/

The young defended it in practice and in theory
  (In theory the more important of the two)
Until they themselves were ancient celebrities, weary
  Of having always to look back at the new.

3/

It had but one aim: to baffle all expectations
  And do whatever it intended to:
When you agreed with it, it snorted with impatience,
  And when you despised it, it agreed with you.

4/

And we, in its wake, cling to whatever keeps us afloat,
  Diminished by our having missed it, though
Man Ray's a consolation: "They say that I missed the boat,
  But all of the boats *I* missed sank years ago."

At Home with Psyche and Eros

Not much of a reader or writer
Himself, but always hot for a good fable,
    Eros has heaped the tabloids that he bought her
On Psyche's coffee table:
    The HOUSEWIFE who is TAKEN UP IN RAPTURE
    Rubs elbows with the ALIENS that CAPTURE
       BIGFOOT'S PREGNANT DAUGHTER!

Having accepted her lover
And his limitations, Psyche still wonders
    Whether a book *can't* be judged by its cover,
As on her chaise she ponders
    The glossy pages of *Panache* or *Flic*
    Till "Beuys at MOMA: A Feminist Critique"
       Glazes her eyes over.

Vain Speculations

What then, if Ri vaThurrison had missed,
When Grozmal, leaping from his brettathurk,
Uncoiled the brindled hydra with a smirk
And fell upon him? Fetid was the mist
That bleared Ri's sight, green tendrils clasped his wrist—
In one sure motion, he unsheathed his dirk
And thrust it home! "My gift has done its work,"
The ancient Hag of Lower Lochmar hissed;

And as Ri stared, her wrinkles fell away
Until his eyes drank in sweet Delia's face!
They mounted Grozmal's 'thurk, and none can say
Where they rode off to, for they left no trace.
But had he missed I'm certain that today
The world would be a very different place.

Still Life with Pears

Hers:
She turns from it and it begins to dry,
An oilslick tightening into the fable
Of a slowly ripening mutuality:
Two pears at rest on the edge of a table.

His:
He wonders if it could ever be the same
As it had been—or was that too a fiction?
He wonders whether this one has a name.
But the third pear is already out of the picture.

To a Snapping Turtle, Lately Hatched

By interrupting your mild gallop
And lifting you, a meager dollop
Of flesh resembling a scallop
          Encrusted with dirt,
I no doubt saved you from a wallop
          That would have hurt;

Eyeball to eyeball now, you blink
And faster than thought (you cannot think)
Reflexively begin to shrink
          Down to a center
Guarded by armor without a chink,
          That naught may enter.

But *one* cannot go into zero:
With too much flesh to disappear, you
Have no choice but play the hero,
          Which you do with grace,
Head jutting out, then limbs—an aero-
          naut, treading space!

So profoundly self-sufficient
You do not even seem to want
A turtle or an elephant
          To stand upon—
No cosmological event
          Holds your attention.

You are perfection of a kind
But cannot know (you would not mind)
How utterly you're left behind.
                    Taking your side,
I put you down before the pond
                    Where you'll reside,

Your destiny, to lie in mud
(And our far more toxic crud)
With your jaws parted to the flood,
                    Wiggling your tongue
Until some darter nips its bud
                    And the trap is sprung;

Or venturing among the shallows
For waterfowl in water-willows,
Gulping a drumstick in two swallows,
                    So great your greed.
You will not boast among your fellows
                    Of my good deed,

But someday on the shore, I'll watch
A line of geese (now out of reach)
Sing your powers of retention, each
                    With one leg missing;
And what they've learned from you, they'll teach,
                    Volubly hissing.

Stanzas after *Endgame*

1/

Hurrying toward a tiny Off-Off-Off-
Off-Broadway theater on the Bowery,
We step around a shouting match of gruff
    Derelicts whose poverty
This Sunday afternoon has found a small
Stage to enact its outrage on, a temporary
    Refuge from the wrecker's ball;

2/

Here artists and their lofts survive by grace
Of our needy city's celebrated
Developers, whose greed for office space
    Seems for now to have abated;
And here men wait with rags and dirty water
To smear new grime on windshields of intimidated
    Drivers who curse, but give a quarter;

3/

Quarters accumulated buy a quart
Of *Gold Coin Extra* or *Lone Star Malt Brew*;
Others do crack or heroin, or snort
    Fumes out of bags of plastic glue;
In the urinous storefronts where they meet,
Nodding acquaintances impatiently renew
    The ties that bind them to the street.

4/

No better place than this to stage a play
That illustrates the way the world will end,

64

For who will come to see it anyway,
    But the subscribers, who attend
Everything? Yet look: pressed against the curb's
Split lip, twin arks—from which, in disbelief descend
    Dazed voyagers from distant suburbs:

5/

Two *Short Line* buses with the audience:
The first is full of high school kids and teachers,
The second carries senior citizens
    Clutching discount ticket vouchers;
    As they negotiate front stairs and aisle,
Purplespiked mutants grimly stalk the blue-rinsed grouches
    Up and into the theater, while

6/

We in the middle find our seats and pray,
Unhopefully, that Beckett's spare precision
Survive all cries of "What did he just say?"
    And adolescent snorts of derision:
    The young with their tongues in one anothers' ears,
And their elders talking back to television,
    Except this isn't television, dears.

7/

The lights go down and we become aware
Of someone on stage, motionless at first,
Beginning to move around a covered chair;
    The way taken is at once reversed:
    Upstage, downstage, dithering left and right,
Until the tiny stage is thoroughly traversed:
    No other characters in sight.

8/

A promising beginning this is not.
From a few rows back comes an angry hiss:
"Isn't it . . . doesn't it . . . hasn't it . . . got a plot?"
     An answer started from across
The aisle is throttled down in someone's throat as
We lean into a vortex of expanding loss,
     That's taken us before we notice;

9/

New characters emerge, the sum of their
Seemingly irreversible reverses:
Hamm (underneath the covers on the chair)
     Joins *Clov* (on stage) and fiercely curses
Progenitor and Genetrix (the droll
Nagg, the winsome *Nell*) then brokenly rehearses
     Life at ground zero of the soul,

10/

Where first there is not enough and then there's more
And more of not enough, insufficiency
In slow addition, grain upon grain before
     It happens ever so suddenly
That insufficiency becomes too much
To bear, absent the hope that there might ever be
     Enough insufficiency, as such.

11/

Once there was something other than what's here,
Which is to say, a time that wasn't now:
Once shape and shapeless played with far and near,
     Motion and stillness, brightness and shadow;
Once there were places variously green

And pools they had, of clear water, wherein we saw
    Ourselves and our selves were seen—

12/

Reflections and expansions of the self!
The past not merely an accumulation!
Progressive toys on every kiddie's shelf!
    But why must we go on and on
About the something more than not enough?
No reason: even as insufficiency, redun-
    dancy, though made of sterner stuff,

13/

Is certainly as equally absurd,
Meaningless, purposeless—yet we attend,
Hang, it is fair to say, on every word
    That brings us nearer to the end
Of stillness and silence. A brief tableau,
Then darkness separates those who must stay behind
    From those who are now free to go.

14/

From this immersion we emerge subdued
And seem more careful of one another;
The elders less cranky and the young not rude
    But helpful as we leave together,
Guiding an elbow, retrieving a dropped cane
For someone old enough to be Adam's grandfather,
    And whom we'll never meet again.

15/

Why are we so changed? Perhaps it's simple:
A parable of Kafka's comes to mind,

Of the leopards who break into the temple
And drink the spirits that they find
In consecrated vessels; their continual
Thefts (being now predictable) are soon assigned
A part within the ritual.

16/

Meaning emerges out of random act
And lasts as long as there are those intent
On finding it and keeping it intact
In fables of impermanence.
We leave the theater as though illustrating
How hard that is to do. The going audience
Begins to board the buses waiting

17/

At curbside to recall them from this dream
Into their lives: the young are making dates,
Their elders trying to remember them.
Slowly, slowly, it separates!
Some are still standing outside the theater,
While others take off briskly down the darkening streets
Wrapped up in their own thought, or

18/

Arguing, like these four on the corner,
About the meaning of it all, before
They set out to find themselves some dinner
At the newly redecorated Hunan Court,
Where many fragrant wonders are provided
Soon for the delectation of one carnivore,
Two vegetarians, one undecided.

Acknowledgments

An early version of "Breaking Old Ground" appeared in *The Threepenny Review* (as "From the Lost and Found"); "Victoria's Secret" appeared in *Hellas;* "Tonight's Jeopardy," in *Arion;* "Souvenirs of the Late War," in *The Epigrammatist;* "A Night at the Opera," in *Poetry (as "Dido and Aeneas");* "Getting the Miracle Wrong," in *Wigwag;* "The Two of Them," "Neither Here Nor There," and "To a Snapping Turtle Lately Hatched," in *The Formalist;* "Reflections after a Dry Spell," in *The Sewanee Theological Review;* "Adolescence" and "At Home with Psyche and Eros," in *Verse;* "Vain Speculations," in *Lemniscate;* "Stanzas after *Endgame,"* in *Boulevard;* "Modernism: The Short Course," in *Janus.*

"Reflections after a Dry Spell" and "The Two of Them" appeared in *Poems for a Small Planet: Contemporary American Nature Poetry.*

Many of these poems first appeared in *Past Closing Time,* a chapbook published by Robert L. Barth of Edgewood, Kentucky.

I am grateful for a Creative Writing Fellowship Grant from the National Endowment for the Arts and for a PSC-CUNY grant which helped me in the completion of this book.

CHARLES MARTIN is the author of four collections of poems, including *Steal the Bacon*, which was nominated for a Pulitzer Prize, and a translation of the poems of Catullus (both available from Johns Hopkins University Press) as well as a critical introduction to the Latin poet's work. His poems have appeared in *Poetry*, the *New Yorker*, the *Hudson Review, Boulevard*, the *Threepenny Review*, and many other magazines and anthologies. He is the recipient of a Bess Hokin Award from *Poetry* and creative writing fellowship grants from the Ingram-Merrill Foundation and the National Endowment for the Arts. A professor at Queensborough Community College (CUNY), he lives in Brooklyn with his wife and one of their two children

Poetry Titles in the Series

John Hollander, *"Blue Wine" and Other Poems*

Robert Pack, *Waking to My Name: New and Selected Poems*

Philip Dacey, *The Boy under the Bed*

Wyatt Prunty, *The Times Between*

Barry Spacks, *Spacks Street: New and Selected Poems*

Gibbons Ruark, *Keeping Company*

David St. John, *Hush*

Wyatt Prunty, *What Women Know, What Men Believe*

Adrien Stoutenberg, *Land of Superior Mirages: New and Selected Poems*

John Hollander, *In Time and Place*

Charles Martin, *Steal the Bacon*

John Bricuth, *The Heisenberg Variations*

Tom Disch, *Yes, Let's: New and Selected Poems*

Wyatt Prunty, *Balance as Belief*

Tom Disch, *Dark Verses and Light*

Thomas Carper, *Fiddle Lane*

Emily Grosholz, *Eden*

X. J. Kennedy, *Dark Horses*

Wyatt Prunty, *The Run of the House*

Robert Phillips, *Breakdown Lane*

Vicki Hearne, *The Parts of Light*

Timothy Steele, *The Color Wheel*

Josephine Jacobsen, *In the Crevice of Time: New and Collected Poems*

Thomas Carper, *From Nature*

John Burt, *Work without Hope*

Charles Martin, *What the Darkness Proposes*